ROCKABYE

CROCODILE

by Jose Aruego and Ariane Dewey

Greenwillow Books, New York

For Juan

Watercolors, gouache paints, and a
black line were used for the full-
color art. The text type is Korinna.

Printed in Singapore
by Tien Wah Press

First Edition

10 9 8 7 6 5 4 3 2 1

**Library of Congress
Cataloging-in-Publication Data**
Aruego, Jose.
Rockabye crocodile.
Summary: Two elderly boars with
contrasting dispositions take turns
caring for a baby crocodile and find
that their attitudes determine how
they are repaid.
[1. Pigs—Fiction.
2. Crocodiles—Fiction.
3. Behavior—Fiction.]
I. Dewey, Ariane. II. Title.
PZ7.A7475Ro   1988   [E]   87-463
ISBN 0-688-06738-7
ISBN 0-688-06739-5 (lib. bdg.)

Two elderly boars lived in the jungle.
They were neighbors.

Amabel was cheerful and kind.   Nettie was mean and selfish.

One morning, Amabel trotted down to the river to fish.
She was humming, HUM HUM HUM, as she passed
a bamboo tree. It swayed to her tune and dropped
two small fish into her basket.
"Why, thank you," she said.

The bamboo replied with a shower of minnows.

Amabel filled her basket, said thank you again, and went on.
She still needed a really big fish to fill her belly.
Suddenly she stumbled over a crocodile.
"OH DEAR!" she cried.

"Good morning, Grandmother," growled the crocodile.
"Why don't you watch where you're going?"
"Excuse me," Amabel said. "I didn't see you. I was
looking for a fish for dinner."

"I'll catch one for you," said the crocodile, "if you'll
do something for me. Come into my cave."

A baby crocodile lay howling in a mud puddle
in a corner of the dark, dirty cave.

"Isn't he sweet?" said the crocodile. "But he won't stop crying. Rock him to sleep and you won't be sorry. I'll be right back." And off she went.

The baby was muddy and cold, but Amabel held him gently and rocked and hummed, rocked and hummed. Soon the baby stopped howling and went to sleep.

The crocodile went to the deepest part of the river and caught some eels and crabs and a very large fish.

Then she wove a basket from river reeds,
filled it, and returned to the cave.

"Here, Grandmother," she said. "Come back whenever you want more fish."

"Thank you, I will," said Amabel. "He's such a nice baby." Then she hurried home.

"Where did you catch all those fish?" Nettie demanded.

"It all started with the bamboo tree," said Amabel.

"And then I met a crocodile."

She told Nettie the whole story while they shared the fish.

Early the next morning Nettie rushed to the river with a huge basket.

She shook the bamboo tree.
"Turn your leaves into fish for me," she ordered.
Nothing happened. She butted the tree hard.

The bamboo snapped back and sent her flying into a
prickle bush.
"OOOUWHA!" she screamed, and ran along the river bank.

"Where's that crocodile and her crybaby?" she snarled.
The crocodile stuck her head out of the cave.
"Oh, there you are," Nettie grunted.
"Go fill this basket with eels, crabs, and big fish.
AND HURRY UP!"

The crocodile was very angry, but she said,
"Rock my baby to sleep and I'll do what you ask."

Nettie grabbed the baby and bounced him up and down.
"What an ugly son. If I had one like you, I'd run," she crooned.
The baby cried harder.

It wasn't long before the crocodile returned. She snatched
back her baby and handed Nettie a basket.
"Don't uncover this basket before you lock your doors
and windows or the fish will escape," she growled.

Nettie grabbed the basket and was out the door
and running home.

"This food is all for me," she decided. "I won't share
even a fish eye with Amabel."

Nettie sneaked into her house and bolted the door. She sealed the windows and stuffed grass into the cracks and holes. Finally she opened the basket.

WOOoooOoosh!

Out came spiders and scorpions, rats and bats.
Nettie huddled in a corner.

Next door, Amabel heard the noise.
"What a ruckus," she thought. "I'd better see what's going on at Nettie's house." Amabel had to break the door down. The spiders, scorpions, rats, and bats rushed out of the open door.

"Oh, Amabel," Nettie cried. "I'm so glad to see you. I've been such a fool."

"Poor Nettie," said Amabel. "Come over to my house and have some tea and tell me all about it."

From that day on, Nettie and Amabel took turns caring for the crocodile baby and the bamboo tree, and the crocodile supplied them with all the fish they could eat.